Lucky
Porcupine!

by MIRIAM SCHLEIN

illustrated by MARTHA WESTON

Four Winds Press   New York

LIBRARY OF CONGRESS CATALOGING IN PUBLICATION DATA

Schlein, Miriam.
  Lucky porcupine!
  SUMMARY: Introduces the physical characteristics,
habits and natural environment of various species of
porcupines.
  1. Porcupines — Juvenile literature. [1. Porcupines]
I. Weston, Martha. II. Title.
QL737.R652S3   599'.3234   79-19673
ISBN 0-590-07543-8

Published by Four Winds Press
A division of Scholastic Magazines, Inc., New York, N.Y.
Printed in the United States of America
Library of Congress Catalog Card Number: 79-19673
1 2 3 4 5 84 83 82 81 80

Lucky
Porcupine !

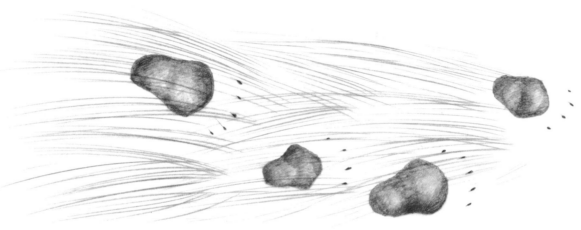

What is that round, fuzzy thing, way up in the tree?
It's not a bird's nest. It's a porcupine.
What is she doing up there?

This is what happened:

A few hours ago, she was walking through the woods. Suddenly she heard something coming. She knew it might be danger. Porcupine doesn't like to fight, and she's not a fast runner. How could she get away?

This is what she did.

She waddled over to a tall tree. She put her short legs around the tree trunk. Slowly, surely, she began to climb.

She's a good climber. She has long, curved claws, to dig into the bark. Her feet have wide bottoms, to grasp the curved trunk. And she uses her tail as she goes up, for balance and support.

When she was high enough up, she stopped, and looked down. The animal chasing her was a dog. He couldn't reach her now. And she knew that he'd go away after a while. So, comfortable and safe, 50 feet above the ground, she went to sleep.

Lucky porcupine, to be such a good climber!

Suppose there had been no tree nearby? What would have happened?

If there were no tree nearby, and if Porcupine had no time to run away, she could have defended herself very well, right there on the ground.

When you see a porcupine waddling along, she may look like just a big soft black-and-white puffball, with lots of long wavy hairs. But don't be fooled. Hidden by these long "guard" hairs on her back and tail are thousands of quills. They are two or three inches long, and sharp as needles. A porcupine has more than 30,000 quills. These are her fighting weapons.

Most of the time, the quills lie flat, hidden among the guard hairs. But if there is danger, or if something just lightly touches her body — sometimes even just a puff of wind — the quills automatically stick right up. Now Porcupine is ready to fight.

She growls and chatters her teeth. She stamps her feet. If the other animal still doesn't go away, this is what Porcupine does. She turns her backside to him. She tucks her face low, hunches her back up, and begins to swing her tail fast, back and forth, back and forth. That strong tail is loaded with quills.

A porcupine is not able to "shoot" her quills. But they are lightly attached, and loose ones will fly out, and hit the dog in the face and chest. If he continues to move in closer and get hit by her tail, or if he tries to bite the porcupine, then he is really in trouble. He will get his face or mouth stuck full of quills.

Quills don't come out easily. They have barbs along the sides, and are hard to pull out. The dog will run home very fast. We hope somebody will pull the quills out for him right away with a pliers.

Poor dog! Do you think he will remember never to go after a porcupine again?

Do you think the porcupine was mean? Remember she did not go after the dog. The dog came after her. How could she know that he would not hurt her, or maybe even try to kill her?

In the wild, the porcupine has many fierce enemies. There is coyote, wolf, cougar, lynx. There is fisher, fox, bear, eagle, owl, and mountain lion. In some parts of the world, there is tiger and panther. All of these are meat eaters. And all of them will go after Porcupine to try and kill her and eat her. An enemy like this is called a "predator."

How can they kill her, if she has her quills to defend herself? How can they get at her?

Porcupine has some weak spots. On her underbody — her belly and beneath her tail—there are no quills. If she is in a tree, some predators, like the fisher, can climb up under her, hit her in the belly, and knock her over. Or, if she is on the ground, a fisher will run around her, quickly stick a paw under her, and flip her over on her back. Lying this way, belly up, she cannot defend herself. The fisher can kill her.

EAGLE

LYNX

OWL

WOLF

COUGAR

FOX

FISHER

BEAR

In winter, if Porcupine is walking on top of the snow, a fisher can burrow under the snow, and attack her from below. The fisher is probably Porcupine's worst enemy.

But even with such fast and fierce and hungry enemies, quite often Porcupine is the winner. And the animal who attacks her may die. This is what happens. The attacking animal may get quills in its face and mouth. If the animal cannot pull the quills out, it will not be able to eat, and will starve to death. Or, if the quills hit some other part of the body, and the animal is not able to pull them out, they can kill in a different way. Slowly, the quills will work their way deeper and deeper into the animal's body. Each day, they will move in about one inch. And if a quill happens to pierce the animal's heart or lungs or liver, it will cause death. Porcupine can kill a bear this way. Or a mountain lion.

All this makes Porcupine sound like a ferocious creature. But is she, really? Really, she is a peaceful thing. She likes to be left alone. She fights only when she is attacked.

Have you ever seen a porcupine out in the woods?
No?

If you haven't, one reason for that might be that they are nocturnal. They are a night animal. At night, when you are sleeping, they are wandering about. In the day, when you

are out, they are usually in their dens, sleeping.

    At some time, you might have walked right past a porcupine and not even seen it. That long, wavy hair going every which way blends in with the weeds and bushes. Even if a porcupine is up in a tree, it is hard to make it out.

But they do leave some clues you can look for.

Look at the base of this tree. There are lots of little sawdusty-looking pellets all around it. These are porcupine droppings. They show that a porcupine has been up there for a while.

Here is a den entrance. How can you tell? Some loose quills have dropped off. They are lying around. And sometimes at the den entrance, you can also notice a strong smell of urine.

Most of the year, Porcupine lives alone. She has more than one den, or home. She may have a den in a hollow log, and another one in a cave. She can also have a burrow under the ground. Sometimes Porcupine will live in an old mine, or under a house where people are living.

In the day, she sleeps in one of her dens. In the night, she comes out and wanders about, looking for food. She makes quite definite porcupine-paths leading from her dens to the feeding areas.

In the spring, she eats buds and twigs and leaves. Later on, she'll eat nuts, fruit, acorns, turnips, mushrooms. She will eat geraniums, if she sees any. She likes wild onions, sunflowers, berries. And she loves carrots. Sometimes she will wade into a pond — holding her tail erect to keep the quills dry — and munch on the lily pads in the water.

Porcupine is a good swimmer. Her quills are hollow. They help keep her afloat. They're a sort of natural life jacket.

Lucky porcupine! She's never without her life jacket!

In the winter, when there is less food on the ground, she spends more time up in trees — even if there is no dog chasing her. She will climb a birch tree, or a pine, or a sugar maple, and gnaw on the inner bark. If she gnaws all around the trunk, the upper part of the tree will die.

If there is a big snowstorm, she may stay up there for weeks. Why should she move? She is comfortable. She has food from the tree. She can sleep up there. And she's not cold, either. In winter, her underfur gets thick, like sheep's wool. It keeps her warm in below-zero weather.

Lucky porcupine, to have such a warm winter coat!

When she does come down, she can burrow under the snow, or she can walk on top of it. If she walks on top, she will leave pigeon-toed footprints and tail marks in the snow.

Now where is she going?
She has decided to go back to her den.

She is not alone in it now. In winter, porcupines no longer live alone. Very often, several of them live together in one den. In winter, they do not wander about as much as they do in summer. And when they do go out, they don't go very far. They may eat some pine needles or bark, and then come back. In winter they do not use several different dens, but stay in one permanent den, with the others.

Porcupines live in most parts of the United States, except for some of the southeastern states. They also live in Alaska and Canada. Porcupines living here are called *North American porcupines.*

There you are, camping in the woods on a summer night. It is hard for you to sleep. Suddenly you hear coughing. Who is it? It is not one of your friends. They are all sleeping. Now you hear moaning. You look around again. Who can it be? It's a little scary.

Now, if this ever happens to you, you will know who it is.
It's no ghost, or mystery person. It's a porcupine.

Porcupines grunt, moan, whine, cough, and make all kinds of noises. And one might be hanging around your camp, because you might have some things that they are very interested in — like lettuce, carrots, nuts, apples. You might have other things that they like even better.

You might wake up, and find that something has gnawed away at your canoe paddle. Or your ax handle. Porcupines love the taste of salt. So they like to chew on your paddle, or your ax handle, or anything that's salty with sweat from your hands.

Hide your paddles from porcupines.

When summer is over, porcupines become very active. They run around a lot. The male porcupines scrap around and chase each other. The female porcupines cry out. They chatter their teeth, and moan and sob. The males answer them.

What's all the excitement about?

It is the mating season. The porcupines are looking for mates.

When a male and female meet, the first thing they do is rub noses. Then they sit, face to face, forepaws touching.

Sometimes, before they mate, they do a special sort of dance. They stand up on their hind feet and tail, facing each other. Then they sway their bodies rhythmically, lifting first one hind leg, then the other. They stay with each other a few days before they mate. After they mate, they part.

About seven months later, in the springtime, porcupine baby is born. His head and body measure about 11 inches long. His baby tail is only about 2½ inches. He weighs about a pound*.

His eyes are open, and he has 8 teeth. Later, when he is grown up, he will have 20. He is born with long black hair. And he has quills. The quills are soft when the baby is born. But they get hard in half an hour.

He can walk, too, in half an hour, though he is still a bit unsteady on his feet. When he is only two days old, he is able to climb a tree.

He drinks milk from his mother for about a month and a half. He can eat other things, too. He gains about a pound a month in weight.

When he is grown up, a North American porcupine usually weighs between 8 and 15 pounds. His head and body will measure around 30 inches. His tail is about another 9 inches or so.

*These measurements, and the measurements that follow are converted to metric on page 42.

Once in a while a male North American porcupine gets
to weigh as much as 40 pounds.

A porcupine keeps on growing his whole life. So if you
see a group of porcupines, the biggest, heaviest-looking one
is probably the oldest.

There were porcupines in the world long before there were people. Thirty-five million years ago, there were porcupines in Europe and South America. In Asia, Africa, and North America, there have been porcupines for two or three or four million years.

The world is still full of porcupines. They live in woods, deserts, jungles.

Porcupines that live in different parts of the world are different from one another.

The biggest type of porcupine lives in Europe and is called the *Crested porcupine*. A large male can weigh as much as 66 pounds. His head and body may measure 32 inches. Add about 6 inches more for the tail.

Crested porcupines live in rocky cracks, or in long underground burrows. Sometimes their burrows are more than 50 feet long. They have escape holes in several places, so they don't get trapped. Sometimes they travel in pairs. And sometimes ten of them will share one burrow.

They have longer quills than North American porcupines. Some of their quills measure 15 inches and more, and are a quarter of an inch thick. When an enemy comes too close, a Crested porcupine will growl, stamp his feet, and rattle his quills. When these long quills rattle against one another, it can sound like a rattlesnake.

These big Crested porcupines are more aggressive fighters than North American porcupines. When they are attacked, they rush at their enemy backward, with their quills erect, and spear him.

A Crested porcupine mother can have two or more babies at a time. The North American porcupine has only one at a time.

Unlike the North American porcupine, Crested porcupines practically never climb trees.

Crested porcupines also live in Africa, Indonesia, and the Philippines.

In China, there are *Brush-tailed porcupines.* You can see how they get their name. Their tail ends in a big bunch of flat, paper-thin quills, and looks just like a brush.

Brush-tailed porcupines are fast runners. Maybe this is because of their light weight. They can be 35 inches long, including the tail — but they weigh only about 5 pounds.

They live in the forests, and make dens under termite mounds and among big tree roots.

Brush-tailed porcupines also live in Africa and Sumatra.

Another kind of porcupine has a tail like a monkey. These are called *Prehensile-tailed porcupines*. Like monkeys, they spend most of their time up in trees. Their tails are strong and long, and are used to grasp branches. That is why they are called "prehensile-tailed." "Prehensile" means having the ability to grasp. Their tails have no quills on them. If an enemy comes near, the Prehensile-tailed porcupine will try to bite him, or hit him with the quills on his back.

These porcupines live in the forests of Mexico, Central America, and South America. If one of them gets hurt and starts to cry, it sounds like a human baby crying.

Sometimes people will call a porcupine a "hedgehog." That is a mistake. A hedgehog has quills. But it is not a porcupine. It is a different kind of animal.

Hedgehogs are smaller. Sometimes they are only 4 or 5 inches long. When they are in danger, they roll up into a ball, tuck their face and legs under their body, and erect their quills. They do not swing their tails, like porcupines.

Hedgehogs live in Africa, Europe, and Asia. There are no wild hedgehogs in America.

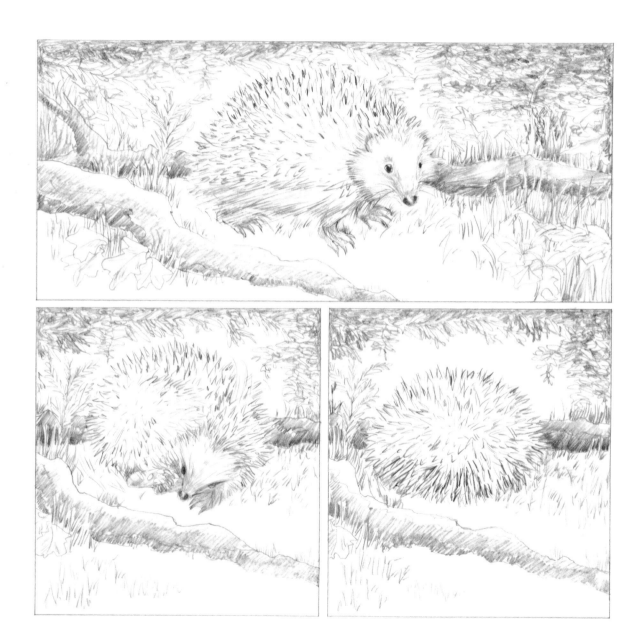

How did the porcupine get its name? The word "porcupine" comes from the Latin language. *Porcus* means pig. And *spina* means thorns. So, a porcupine is a *pig with thorns.*

Do you think that is a good name? The quills or spines are the thorns. But why "pig"? Maybe it is because porcupines have a flat, piglike snout. Or maybe it is because they sometimes make grunting, piglike sounds.

Porcupine — The Pig With Thorns.

Lucky porcupine — not to know that we have given you such a silly name!

IN METRIC TERMS

Page 30
11 inches = about 28 centimeters
2½ inches = about 6 centimeters
1 pound = a bit less than ½ kilogram
Between 8 and 15 pounds =
between 3½ and 7 kilograms
30 inches = about 76 centimeters
9 inches = about 23 centimeters

Page 31
40 pounds = about 18 kilograms

Page 32
66 pounds = about 30 kilograms
32 inches = about 81 centimeters
6 inches = about 15 centimeters
50 feet = about 15 meters
15 inches = about 38 centimeters
¼ inch = about 6 millimeters

Page 34
35 inches = about 89 centimeters
5 pounds = about 2¼ kilograms